For Matt and Mae; my heart and soul.

– Courtney

To Malena & Avery

My greatest teachers and snuggle buddies.

Thank you for choosing me.

– Natalie

Published by Gnat & Corky 2021

ISBN 978-1-7349153-8-9 Hardcover
Library of Congress Control Number: 2021918154

The Ladybug Club
Written by Courtney Kotloski
Illustrated by Natalie Sorrentino

Brookfield, WI

www.gnatandcorky.com

The Ladybug Club

Snuggle Books by Gnat & Corky

Written by Courtney Kotloski • Illustrated by Natalie Sorrentino

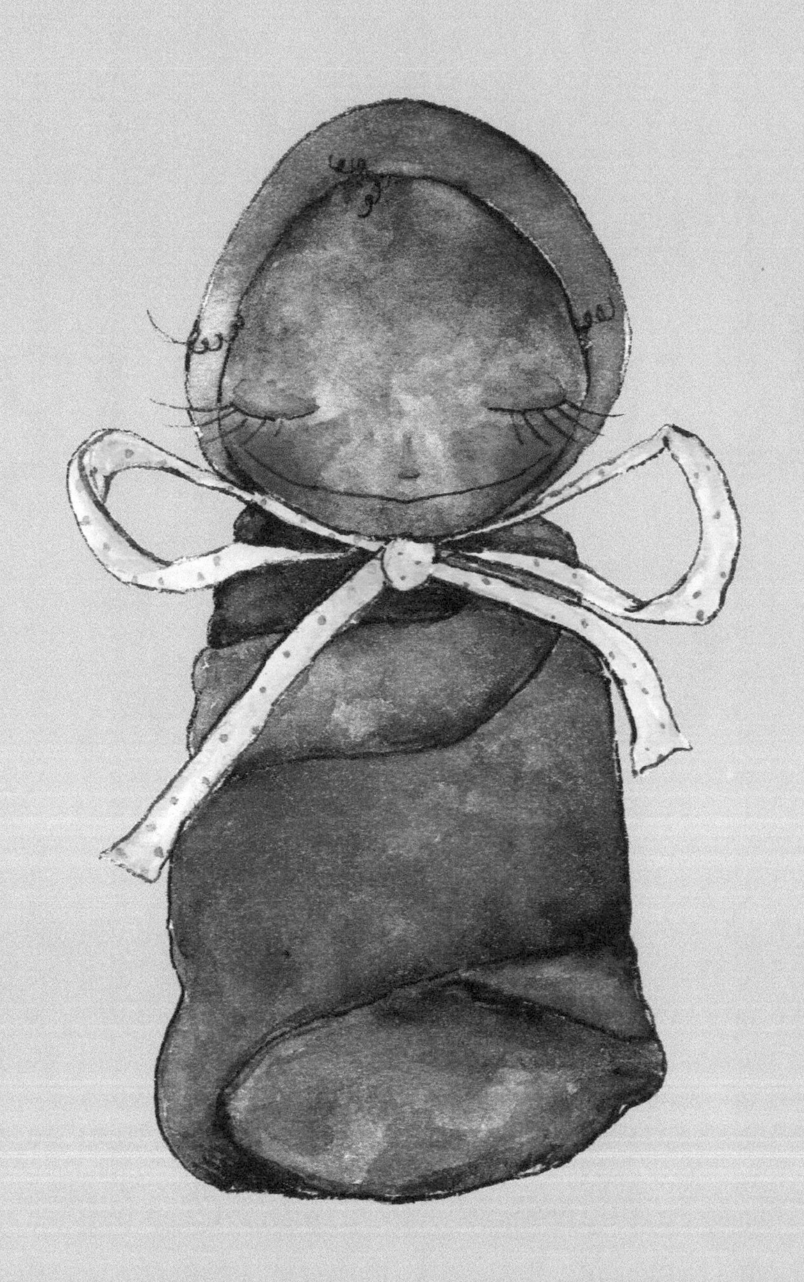

one dot

for the day

we took you

home.

two dots

for your

first bath.

three dots

for that smile
that made nana

laugh.

four dots

for that

tiny

little

tooth.

five dots

for the night

you slept

all the way

through.

six dots

for crawling

across

the

room.

seven dots

for pointing

to the

moon.

eight dots

for standing

on your

own.

nine dots

for giving us

the greatest

joy

we've ever known.

ten dots

for "mama."

eleven dots

for

"dad."

And a new pair of

ladybug wings

for the most

beautiful gift

the world could have.

Welcome to the

Ladybug Club!

Thank you for the snuggle.

Did you know you can visit our website and answer
our questions? We read every submission, and our
Gnat & Corky Book series is based on real kids just like you.
Check out more book titles and products and send us a
message at www.gnatandcorky.com.

We love hearing from our readers!

CPSIA information can be obtained
at www.ICGtesting.com
Printed in the USA
BVHW021149061021
618279BV00004B/106